DISCARDED BY
SAYVILLE LIBRARY

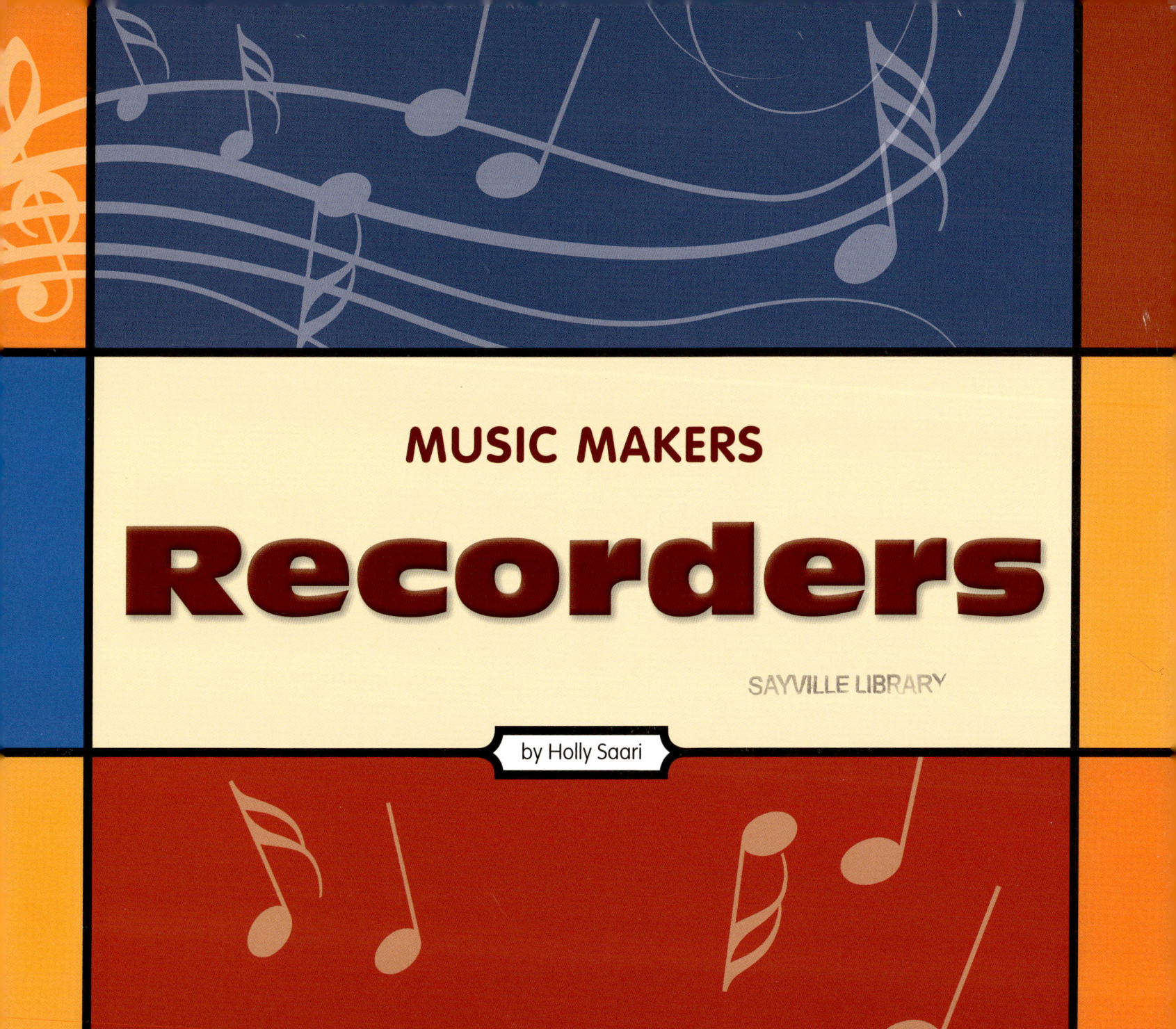

MUSIC MAKERS: RECORDERS

Watch her fingers cover the holes. Hear the whistle sounds fill the air. She is playing the recorder.

A girl plays the recorder.

The recorder is a kind of flute. A flute is a **woodwind** instrument. Air flows through the recorder and **vibrates** to make a sound.

Air flows through the recorder's body.

A recorder has a mouthpiece called a **fipple**. It is like a whistle. Air blown through it makes whistling sounds.

The player's mouth rests on the fipple.

The recorder has seven holes on the front. One hole is on the back for the thumb. The player's fingers cover and uncover the holes to make notes.

A player practices covering the finger holes.

MUSIC MAKERS: RECORDERS

A recorder can make many notes. Some are high and some are low. Blowing more air into the recorder makes a louder sound.

A recorder player has to practice.

A player holds a recorder in front of herself. The bottom points toward the ground.

A recorder points toward the ground.

MUSIC MAKERS: RECORDERS

Recorders are made from wood or plastic. Most are about the length of a **forearm**.

Recorders are made in different lengths.

Recorders were very **popular** in Europe during the **Middle Ages**. However, they are still played all over the world.

A recorder can be played with another instrument.

Many children play recorders in school. They learn about them in music class.

Children play recorders in their classroom.

MUSIC MAKERS: RECORDERS

Toot, toot. Whistle, whistle. Playing the recorder is so much fun!

The recorder can be practiced outside.

Glossary

fipple (FIH-pull): A fipple is the mouthpiece of a recorder. A player puts his or her mouth on the fipple.

forearm (FOR-arm): The forearm is the part of the arm from the wrist to the elbow. Some recorders are the length of a forearm.

Middle Ages (MID-ull AY-jez): The Middle Ages are the period of history in Europe from the 400s to the 1400s. Recorders were often played during the Middle Ages.

popular (POP-yuh-ler): Something that is popular is liked by many people. Recorders were popular in Europe.

vibrates (VY-brayts): Something that moves back and forth very quickly vibrates. Air vibrates when it is blown through a recorder.

woodwind (WOOD-wind): A woodwind is a type of instrument that is, or used to be, made from wood. The recorder is a woodwind.

To Find Out More

Books

Hutton, Eric. *Music Magic: Play the Recorder*. San Diego, CA: Silver Dolphin Books, 2006.

Storey, Rita. *The Recorder and Other Wind Instruments*. North Mankato, MN: Smart Apple Media, 2009.

Thomas, John E. *Music in Minutes: Recorder*. New York: Sterling, 2005.

Web Sites

Visit our Web site for links about recorders: *childsworld.com/links*

Note to Parents, Teachers, and Librarians: We routinely verify our Web links to make sure they are safe and active sites. So encourage your readers to check them out!

Index

fipple, 6
flute, 4
holes, 2, 8
length, 14
Middle Ages, 16
notes, 8, 10
school, 18
sound, 4, 6, 10
whistle, 2, 6, 20

About the Author

Holly Saari enjoys contributing to children's education through the written word. She's an avid reader and also likes to practice playing the piano.

On the cover: A girl practices the recorder.

Published by The Child's World®
1980 Lookout Drive • Mankato, MN 56003-1705
800-599-READ • www.childsworld.com

ACKNOWLEDGMENTS
The Child's World®: Mary Berendes, Publishing Director
The Design Lab: Design and production
Red Line Editorial: Editorial direction

PHOTO CREDITS: Susan Stewart/iStockphoto, cover, 15; iStockphoto, cover, 13; Karen Town/iStockphoto, 3; Heath Doman/iStockphoto, 5; Carrie Bottomley/iStockphoto, 7; Nola Rin/Shutterstock, 9; Bronwyn Photo/Shutterstock, 11; Ramona S/Shutterstock, 17; Morgan Lane Photography/Shutterstock, 19; Mark Rose/iStockphoto, 21

Copyright © 2010 by The Child's World®
All rights reserved. No part of this book may be reproduced or utilized in any form or by any means without written permission from the publisher.

Printed in the United States of America in Mankato, Minnesota.
November 2009
F11460

LIBRARY OF CONGRESS CATALOGING-IN-PUBLICATION DATA
Saari, Holly.
  Recorders / by Holly Saari.
    p. cm. — (Music makers)
  Includes index.
  ISBN 978-1-60253-356-1 (library bound : alk. paper)
 1. Recorder (Musical instrument)—Juvenile literature. I. Title. II. Series.
ML990.R4S23 2010
788.3'619—dc22   2009030208

SAYVILLE LIBRARY
88 GREENE AVENUE
SAYVILLE, NY 11782

OCT 2 1 2019